Read, talk, and play with your child everyday
Lea, hable y juege con su niño cada día

Tortillas and Lullabies

Tortillas y cancioncitas

Tortillas and Lullabies
Tortillas y cancioncitas

BY
LYNN REISER

PICTURES BY "CORAZONES VALIENTES"
COORDINATED AND TRANSLATED BY REBECCA HART

GREENWILLOW BOOKS
An Imprint of HarperCollinsPublishers

rayo

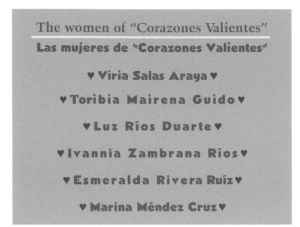

The women of "Corazones Valientes"
Las mujeres de "Corazones Valientes"

♥ Viria Salas Araya ♥

♥ Toribia Mairena Guido ♥

♥ Luz Ríos Duarte ♥

♥ Ivannia Zambrana Ríos ♥

♥ Esmeralda Rivera Ruíz ♥

♥ Marina Méndez Cruz ♥

With thanks to John Forster for his help in arranging the lullaby

Consultants on Translation:
Nancy Moscoso-Guzmán, Librarian,
Fair Haven Library, New Haven, Connecticut;
Kay Hill, Ph.D., Supervisor of Foreign Languages,
New Haven Public Schools, New Haven, Connecticut;
Graziella Patrucco de Solodow, artist and teacher of children's book illustration;
Joseph B. Solodow, Ph.D., Chairman, Department of Foreign Languages,
Southern Connecticut State University, New Haven, Connecticut; and
Meneca Turconi, Librarian, Yale Medical Library, New Haven, Connecticut

Rayo is an imprint of HarperCollins Publishers.

Tortillas and Lullabies, Tortillas y cancioncitas
Text copyright © 1998 by Lynn Whisnant Reiser
Illustrations copyright © by "Corazones Valientes"
All rights reserved. Manufactured in China.
www.harpercollinschildrens.com

Acrylic paints were used for the full-color art.
The text type is Kuenstler 480 and Novel Gothic-Normal.

First Rayo edition, 2008

Library of Congress Cataloging-in-Publication Data
Reiser, Lynn. Tortillas and lullabies, tortillas y cancioncitas / by Lynn Reiser;
pictures by "Corazones Valientes"; coordinated and translated by Rebecca Hart.
   p. cm.
"Greenwillow Books"
Summary: A young girl describes activities that her great-grandmother,
grandmother, and mother all did for their daughters, and that she does
for her doll.
ISBN 978-0-688-14628-3 (trade bdg.)
ISBN 978-0-06-089185-5 (pbk.)
[1. Mothers and daughters—Fiction.
2. Spanish language materials—Bilingual.]
I. Hart, Rebecca. II. Corazones Valientes (Organization).
III. Title   PZ73.R42   1998   [E]—dc21
97-7096 CIP AC

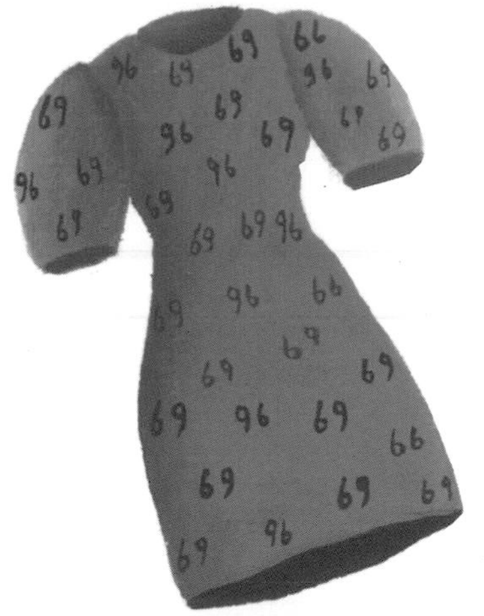

CONTENTS
SUMARIO

1 Tortillas page 6

Tortillas página 6

2 Flowers page 14

Flores página 14

3 Washing page 22

Lavado página 22

4 Lullabies page 30

Cancioncitas página 30

Author's Note page 38

Nota de la autora página 39

One

1

Uno

Tortillas

My great-grandmother made tortillas
for my grandmother;

Mi bisabuela hacía tortillas
para mi abuela;

my grandmother made tortillas
for my mother;

mi abuela hacía tortillas
para mi mamá;

my mother made tortillas for me;

mi mamá hacía tortillas para mí;

and I made tortillas for my doll.

y yo hacía tortillas para mi muñeca.

Every time it was the same, but different.

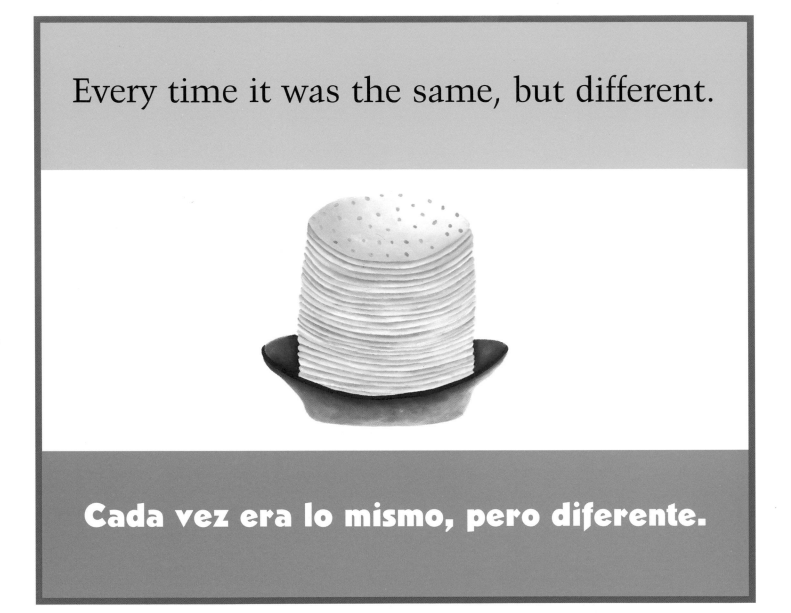

Cada vez era lo mismo, pero diferente.

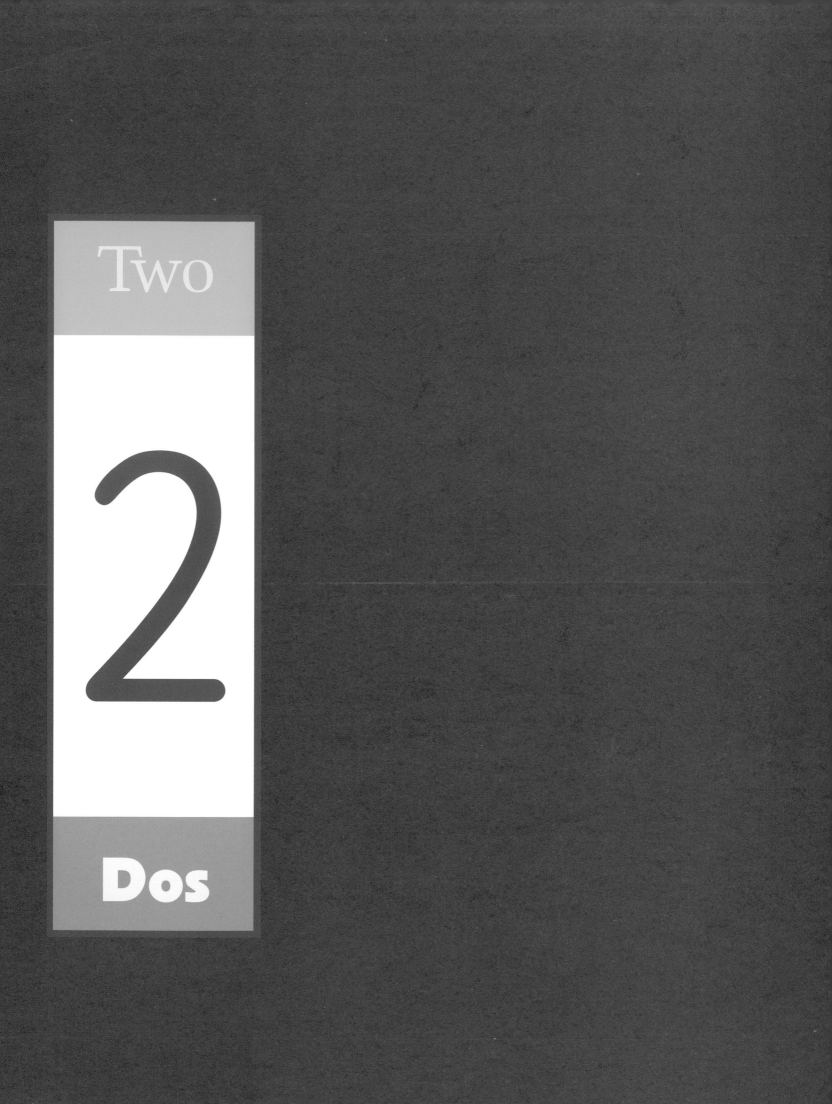

Two

2

Dos

Flowers

Flores

My grandmother gathered flowers
for my great-grandmother;

Mi abuela recogía flores
para mi bisabuela;

my mother gathered flowers
for my grandmother;

mi mamá recogía flores
para mi abuela;

I gathered flowers for my mother;

yo recogía flores para mi mamá;

and my doll gathered flowers for me.

y mi muñeca recogía flores para mí.

Every time it was the same, but different.

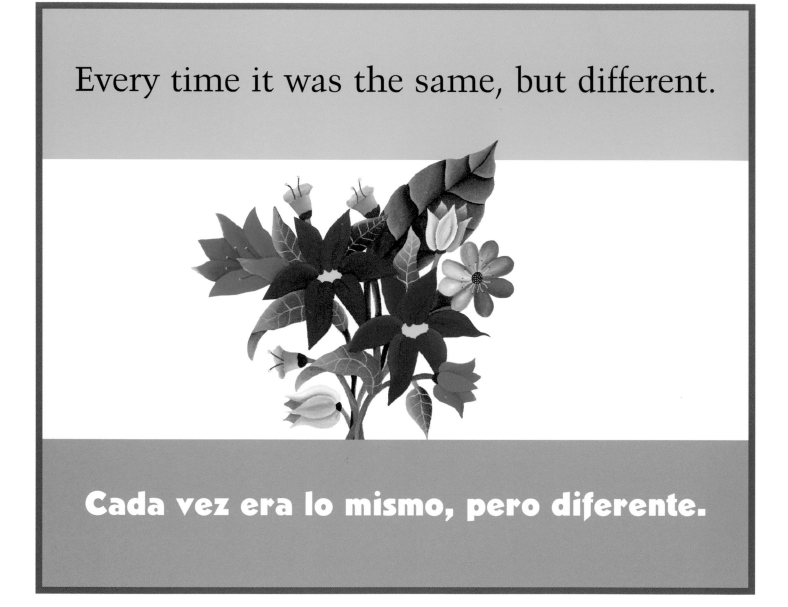

Cada vez era lo mismo, pero diferente.

Three

Washing

Lavado

My great-grandmother washed a dress
for my grandmother;

Mi bisabuela lavaba un vestido
para mi abuela;

my grandmother washed a dress
for my mother;

mi abuela lavaba un vestido
para mi mamá;

my mother washed a dress for me;

mi mamá lavaba un vestido para mí;

and I washed a dress for my doll.

y yo lavaba un vestido para mi muñeca.

Every time it was the same, but different.

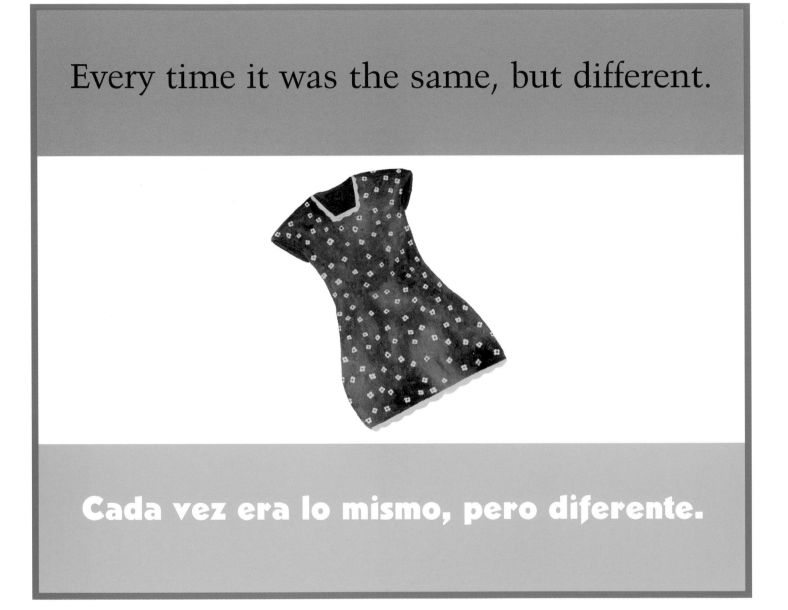

Cada vez era lo mismo, pero diferente.

Four

4

Cuatro

Lullabies

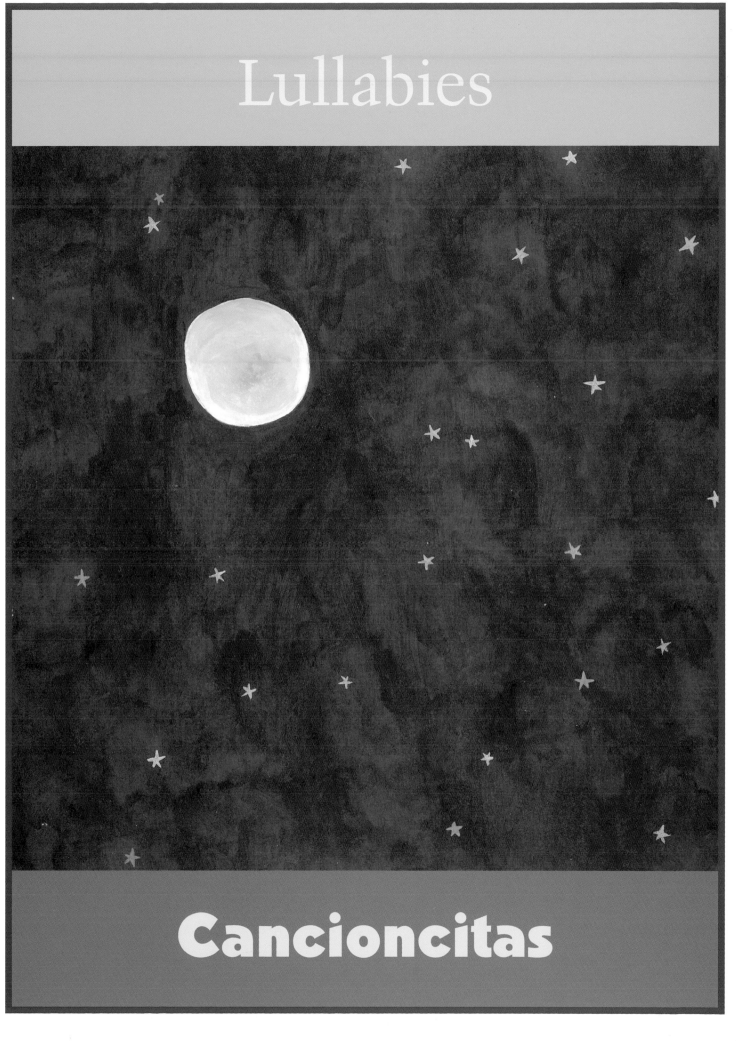

Cancioncitas

My great-grandmother sang a lullaby
to my grandmother;

Mi bisabuela le cantaba una cancioncita
a mi abuela;

my grandmother sang a lullaby
to my mother;

mi abuela le cantaba una cancioncita
a mi mamá;

my mother sang a lullaby to me;

mi mamá me cantaba una cancioncita a mí;

and I sang a lullaby to my doll—

y yo le cantaba una cancioncita a mi muñeca—

and every time it was the same.

y cada vez fue lo mismo.

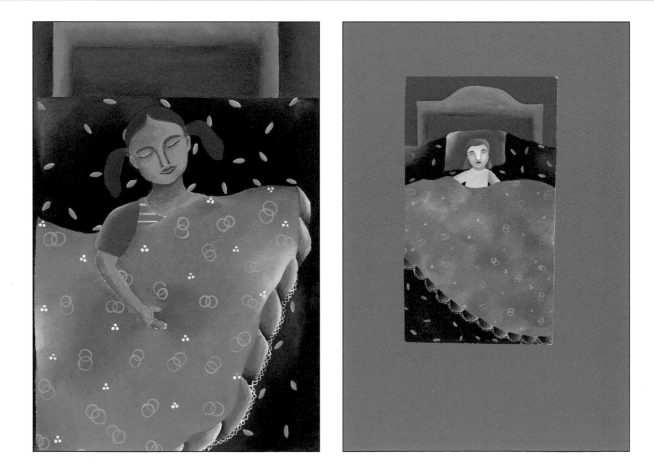

Lullaby

Cancioncita

TRADITIONAL / TRADICIONAL

Hush, hush, lit – tle one, there are things I have to do,___

A – rru – rrú, ni – ñi – ta, que ten – go que ha – cer,___

wash–ing out your dress – es and then sit – ting down to sew.___

la – var los ves - ti – dos y sen – tar – me a co – ser.___

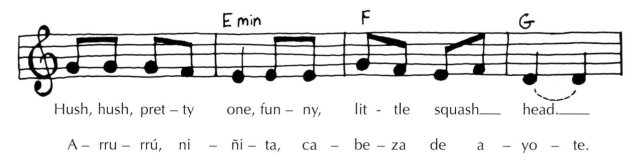

Hush, hush, pret – ty one, fun – ny, lit – tle squash___ head.___

A – rru – rrú, ni – ñi – ta, ca – be – za de a – yo – te.

The coy – ote will eat you if you don't jump in bed.___

Que si no te duer – mes, te come – rá el co – yo – te.

AUTHOR'S NOTE

While writing *Cherry Pies and Lullabies*, a book about a family like mine, I talked with Isabel, my friend from El Salvador, about my family and her family, about making pies and making tortillas. In talking, I came upon the idea of *Tortillas and Lullabies*, *Tortillas y cancioncitas*, a book about a family like Isabel's.

I found the artists for this book at an exhibit of paintings showing life in a Costa Rican farming village. When Isabel saw the paintings, they reminded her so much of home that she began to cry.

The show had been organized by Rebecca Hart, a Peace Corps volunteer in Costa Rica from 1989 to 1992. Rebecca first taught organic gardening to the women of the village. After a year they said, "Rebecca, we are grateful—but isn't there something we could do in the shade?"

So once a week Rebecca traveled by foot and bus to San José to take art lessons, and returned to teach the women to paint. In this way began the careers of the "Corazones Valientes" ("Valiant Hearts"), six women ranging in age from 19 to 42 years who now have exhibited widely in both Costa Rica and the United States.

For the illustrations in *Tortillas and Lullabies*, *Tortillas y cancioncitas*, Viria Salas, Toribia Mairena Guido, Luz Ríos Duarte, Ivannia Zambrana Ríos, Esmeralda Rivera Ruíz, and Marina Méndez Cruz worked together, agreeing upon the contents of the illustrations and sharing the painting. Their art celebrates their heritage, their rapidly changing lives, and the enduring expressions of love in their families in ways that are the same but different.

NOTA DE LA AUTORA

Al escribir <u>Cherry Pies and Lullabies</u>, un libro sobre una familia como la mía, hablé con Isabel, mi amiga de El Salvador, sobre mi familia y su familia, sobre cocinar pasteles de cereza y cocinar tortillas. Mientras hablábamos, me vino la idea para <u>Tortillas and Lullabies, Tortillas y cancioncitas</u>, un libro sobre una familia como la de Isabel. Las artistas que han ilustrado este libro las encontré en una exhibición de cuadros señalando la vida en una aldea agrícola costarricense. Cuando Isabel vió los cuadros, le hicieron recordar tanto de su hogar que comenzó a llorar.

Esta exhibición fue organizada por una voluntaria del Cuerpo de Paz, Rebecca Hart, quien estuvo en Costa Rica desde 1989 hasta 1992. Al comienzo de su estadía, Rebecca enseñó a las mujeres de la aldea la agricultura ecológica. Después de un año éstas dijeron: "Rebecca, estamos muy agradecidas—pero, ¿no podrías encontrar otra cosa que hacer en la sombra?"

Entonces cada semana Rebecca, a pie y en autobús, iba a la ciudad de San José para tomar lecciones en bellas artes y regresaba para enseñar a su vez a las mujeres dibujar y pintar. Así comenzaron las carreras de los "Corazones Valientes", seis mujeres de 19 a 42 años quienes hoy en dia han exhibido en muchos lugares de Costa Rica y los Estados Unidos.

Las ilustraciones para <u>Tortillas and Lullabies, Tortillas y cancioncitas</u> fueron hechas por Viria Salas, Toribia Mairena Guido, Luz Ríos Duarte, Ivannia Zambrana Ríos, Esmeralda Rivera Ruíz, y Marina Méndez Cruz, quienes al ponerse de acuerdo en el contenido de las ilustraciones compartieron el trabajo de pintarlas. Su arte hace homenaje a su patrimonio cultural, su rápido cambio de costumbres y la constancia duradera de expresiones de amor en sus familias, en formas que a la vez se mantienen y se alteran.

GREAT-GRANDMOTHER'S HOUSE ▼ **LA CASA DE LA BISABUELA**

GRANDMOTHER'S HOUSE ▼ **LA CASA DE LA ABUELA**

MOTHER'S HOUSE ▼ **LA CASA DE LA MADRE**

▼▼▼▼▼

To Isabel and her daughters,
Laura and Sara Inez —L. R.

*A Isabel y sus hijas,
Laura y Sara Inez* —L. R.

▼▼▼▼▼

To our ancestors, who have taught us
how to live simply and beautifully.
Thanks to them, we have become
hardworking and honest people.
In gratitude to them, we dedicate
this book. —"C. V."

*A nuestros antepasados, quienes
nos han enseñado a tener una
vida sencilla y hermosa. Gracias
a ellos, hemos llegado a ser personas
trabajadoras y honradas. En
agradecimiento a ellos, les
dedicamos este libro.* —"C. V."

▼▼▼▼▼

To Doña Julia, Don Quincho,
Mrs. Garza, Uncle Phil, Aunt Rebec,
Aunt Janet, Mo Sweney, and
Tom Hart, who have inspired me
with their lives and their gifts
of caring and of laughter —R. H.

*A Doña Julia, Don Quincho, Señora
Garza, Tío Phil, Tía Rebec, Tía Janet,
Mo Sweney, y Tom Hart, quienes
me han inspirado con sus vidas y
sus dones de cariño y risa* —R. H.

▼▼▼▼▼